Joshua Tree National Park

Animals & Attractions

Billy Grinslott & Kinsey Marie Books

ISBN - 9781965098219

The chipmunk is small and bushy tailed. They live in many places in America. Chipmunks are small members of the squirrel family. They have pouches inside of their cheeks so they can carry food. They are very friendly and will take food from your hand.

White Tailed Antelope Squirrel Looks a lot like a chipmunk. They also have pouches inside their mouth to carry food. The difference is they are omnivorous. Meaning, they feed on foliage, seeds, insects, lizards and rodents. Chipmunks typically don't eat meat, but the Antelope Squirrel will eat lizards and rodents. They also live in dryer climates like, deserts and foothills.

Ground squirrels live in burrows which they dig with their sharp claws and muscular legs. Unlike other squirrels they have adapted to living in treeless areas. They will climb trees if there is any in the area. Ground squirrels are one of the largest squirrel species. They grow up to a length of around 17 to 21 inches. Squirrels are important plant dispersers. They gather seeds and nuts and bury them in the dirt, which grows new plants.

Mojave Pocket Gopher got its name because they live in holes in dryer climates. Pocket gophers don't eat outside their burrows and spend approximately 90% of their lives beneath the ground. Pocket gophers can run backwards as fast as they can run forward. They use their bare tail as a feeler when backing up in their burrows. Their loose skin lets them turn a somersault in the tunnel for a quick getaway.

Mojave Round-tailed Ground Squirrel, as you can see, they have a long slender tail. They live underground for most of the year. This ground squirrel is active above ground during the spring and early summer. During the remainder of the summer they aestivate, meaning they are dormant, in burrows constructed near the base of large shrubs.

The Desert Kangaroo Rat got its name because it hops on two legs like a kangaroo. The kangaroo rat is perfectly adapted to life in the desert. They can survive without drinking any water, getting needed moisture from their seed diet. They have excellent hearing and can detect the sound of a flying owl approaching. Kangaroo rats have long tails and large hind feet. Their eyes are large, and their ears are small.

Desert Cottontail are adapted to various habitats from grasslands to cactus deserts. The Desert cottontail is a common species of cottontail rabbit native to North America. The Desert cottontail has large ears that usually stand up straight. It has a greyish-brown, rounded tail with a broad white edge, which is visible as it runs away. Desert cottontails are found throughout the Western United States from eastern Montana to western Texas and in Northern and Central Mexico.

The black tailed jackrabbits most identifying feature is its huge ears. The ears along with the tail are tipped with black fur. Black-tailed jackrabbits are not actually rabbits but are hares. Hares are born with fur and are larger than rabbits. They usually have longer hind legs and ears. These speedy animals can reach speeds of 40 miles an hour. They have powerful hind legs and can jump 10 feet in one jump.

Joshua Tree has 46 different species of reptiles including lizards. Some of the most seen lizards are desert spiny lizards. Lizards feed on a variety of insects including ants, beetles, and caterpillars, spiders, centipedes. Lizards prefer sparsely vegetated rocky areas and shrub-covered dirt banks near water or flowing streams.

Snakes are less commonly seen but 26 species live in the park. Rattlesnakes alone account for seven of the snake species. Its always best to stay away from snakes, because some of them are poisonous. There are more than 3,000 species of snakes on the planet. Snakes have been around for 142 million years They like to hide around rocks, plants and bushy areas. So be careful when hiking in these areas.

There are many birds in Joshua Tree. One of the coolest birds is the Roadrunner. They like to run instead of flying, because they have weak wings compared to their strong legs. They are fast runners. They can run up to 15 miles per hour, with much faster spurts when it needs to. They like to live in deserts, and open country with scattered brush. The road runner got its name, because it likes to hunt for insects along roads and it can be seen running by or on roads.

Mojave desert tortoises can live 60 years in the wild, and sometimes up to 80 years in a zoo. Typically they are found in creosote bush, where scattered shrubs provide abundant space for growth of grasses and wildflowers, the favored foods of the tortoise. They spend about 95% of their lives living in burrows. Tortoises travel long distances in search of food and water and will cross highways through their territory.

Weasels are the smallest members of the meat-eating animals. Although small, they do not hibernate and are active all winter. Weasels have long whiskers like cats, to help them feel things. They even have long whiskers on their elbows. When a weasel gets annoyed, it stomps its feet, just like humans do. Weasels are quick, agile, and alert animals. They are excellent climbers and swimmers.

Badgers live underground with other family members. Badgers are very social and live in groups. A badger den or sett can be centuries old and are used by many generations of badgers. Badgers are very territorial, it's best not to bother them is you see one.

Ringtails look like a racoon. They have stripes on their tails, but their face more resembles a cat. They are a member of the racoon family. Ringtails can be found in the south and southwestern parts of America. Ringtails are excellent climbers capable of ascending vertical walls, trees, rocky cliffs and even cactus. They are mostly nocturnal.

Pee-ewe what is that stinky critter with the big bushy tail. It smells bad. Skunks are normally curious and friendly unless you scare them. If you scare them, they will flip their bushy tale at you and spray you with a smelly potion and it stinks. They will usually warn you before spraying you by bouncing up and down on their front feet. Spotted Skunks look a little different from other skunks. Spotted skunks have a pattern of spots and broken lines, while striped skunks have two white stripes running from head to tail.

The gray fox can be identified by its coat color which is silver-gray on its back and face, reddish on its legs and chest and white on its throat, mid-belly, and the insides of it legs. The gray fox is the only member of the dog family that will climb trees, to sleep, or to escape from predators. They have strong, hooked claws that enable them to climb trees.

The Kit Fox is the smallest species of fox in North America. Despite their slender size, they have large ears to help aid their hearing and to dissipate heat. The kit fox lives in the open desert, on creosote bush flats, and amongst the sand dunes. The desert kit fox is nocturnal, meaning they come out at night. They spend their days living underground in elaborate burrows. Their burrows range from 3 to 6 meters deep, and have multiple entrances.

The coyote is bigger than a fox. Eastern coyotes are part wolf. Coyotes are great for pest control. They like to eat mice and rats. They can adapt and live almost anywhere, even in the city. They have a yip type of call when they communicate with each other. Coyotes are found in all the United States, except Hawaii.

The Lynx is larger than its relative the bobcat and has lighter fur and more spots than a bobcat. The lynx is more than twice the size of a house cat. Lynx have natural snowshoes for feet. Lynx hunt at night. Their tufted ears help to enhance hearing.

The mountain lion is one of the biggest cats in North America. The largest mountain lion ever recorded weighed 276 pounds. Mountain lions don't roar like other big cats they communicate in different ways, such as chirping, growling, shrieking, and even purring. The mountain lion is also known as the cougar.

Black bears are the smallest members of the bear family in North America. Black Bears love to eat sweet things like berries, fruits, and vegetables. They are good climbers and fast runners. They usually sleep for long periods of time and hibernate during the winter.

Mule deer get their name because of their mulelike ears. Male deer are called bucks and females are does. Males grow new antlers every year. They can run 30 miles per hour. They are bigger than whitetail deer and prefer living in the mountain areas.

Desert Bighorn sheep are highly adapted for desert climates and can go for extended periods of time without drinking water. They are social animals and form herds that are usually 8 to 10 sheep. Males will challenge each other and slam their heads together, that's how they got their name ram. Their horns can weigh up to 30 pounds.

If you only have the chance for one short hike, Hidden Valley is a great choice. The Hidden Valley Trail is a one-mile loop hike through a scenic valley surrounded by large rock formations. The trail is excellent for families and offers exciting opportunities for rock scrambling. Along the trail are educational signs about local plants and animals. The trail is considered easy but there are stairs and rock steps at the beginning and ending of the trail.

Stroll through the Cholla Cactus Garden along a flat 0.25-mile loop trail. Hike through thousands of cholla cactus and enjoy scenic mountain views. The Cholla Cactus Garden is in a transition zone between the Colorado and Mojave Deserts. Tread cautiously around these cacti because the cholla segments can break off and attach to people and animals with sharp spines. Wear closed-toed shoes on this trail to protect your feet.

Keys View, this popular destination is perched on the crest of the Little San Bernardino Mountains. It provides awesome panoramic views of the Coachella Valley. It is well worth the 20-minute drive from park boulevard down keys view road. The lookout is wheelchair accessible, or you can hike the .2-mile-loop trail up the ridge for more spectacular views.

Ryan Mountain is a difficult three mile out and back hike with 1,050 feet of elevation gain. The first section of the trail is relatively flat, but quickly gains in elevation up the mountain. This is one of the most popular hikes as it provides sweeping panoramic views of the park. Ryan Mountain is 5,457 feet tall and sits right in the middle of Joshua Tree Park. It offers panoramic views as far as the eye can see. The summit rewards hikers with one of the best 360-degree views of any trail in the park.

Explore the rocky desert landscape on the Barker Dam Trail. An easy 1.1-mile loop trail. Hike through the iconic monzogranite boulders, Joshua trees, and past the historic Barker dam. Visit a rock art site and experience the beauty of the park from a distance. Encounter wildlife big and small, scramble over boulders, and walk along desert washes. Catch a glimpse of the far-off San Gorgonio Mountain. View the plant life in the Mojave Desert, including Joshua trees, creosote, Mojave yucca, pinon pines, and more.

Skull rock got its name because when you look at it, it looks like it has 2 carved out eyes and a carved-out nose. Skull Rock is a favorite stop for park visitors. A parking spot is located just across the road from the rock. For those wishing to hike, a 1.7-mile nature trail begins just across from the entrance to Jumbo rocks campground or inside the campground, across from the amphitheater.

The 49 palms oasis trail. This oasis is a sensitive biological area, as this is a crucial water supply for plant and wildlife. In the early 1900s, miners planted palm trees here to mark where the spring was located. There is a point about 2 miles in when you round a corner of the trail and see the palm trees, and it literally is an oasis. Beautiful palm trees in the middle of the desert. The hike is 3 miles round trip and requires some moderate hiking. But it is well worth it!

Take a ranger-led tour and learn about the cultural history of Keys Ranch. Topics include Native American history, mining, ranching, homesteading, the Keys family, and the site's protected history. The property is in a remote, rocky canyon. To preserve its historic character, admission to the ranch is restricted to guided half mile walking tours. Group size is limited. Tours are typically held from October through May. Tickets are required and can be reserved ahead of time.

The Arch Rock Trailhead looks like a lollipop. the route heads in a straight line for about .6 miles from the parking lot to the east, where it becomes a short loop. Hiking it counterclockwise is recommended because it is easier to spot the arch from that direction. The loop is a short .2 miles and leads hikers back to the straightaway trail to the parking lot. Arch Rock is a popular attraction, so you might choose to visit early in the day to avoid crowds. It offers views of Arch Rock, Whale Rock, and a short detour to Heart Rock.

Cap Rock Trail. This trail is a 0.4-mile loop with minimal elevation change. It winds through the Joshua tree woodland and spectacular monzogranite rock formations. You will get to view Juniper woodlands, as well as a spectacular diversity of desert shrubs. Cap Rock trail is a short, flat, easy nature trail that is appropriate for everyone. Cap Rock Nature Trail offers a captivating glimpse into the park's unique ecosystem.

The Wonderland of Rocks is a backcountry area that is a maze of rock and boulder piles. The Wonderland of Rocks is a 12-square-mile maze of massive, granite rock formations. Proceed cautiously on this 5.5-mile point to point trail. Generally considered a highly challenging route. It is also possible to get lost in this area because the trails wind through the rock formations.

Lost Horse mine is a popular destination for visitors looking for a moderate hike. The trail, which is a four-mile round-trip, follows the road. Mine shafts are dangerous, and historic structures are easily damaged. While the Lost Horse site has been stabilized, it is still not safe to walk on. Lost Horse Mine operated from 1893 to 1936, producing over 9,000 ounces of gold. It was one of the most successful mines in the Joshua Tree National Park area.

Split Rock Loop Trail is a 2.5-mile loop hike with 150 feet of elevation gain. On the trail, you'll see scenic views of the unique rock formations, the jumbo rocks area, and wide-open desert views. If you're looking for a scenic spot to have lunch, there is picnic tables near the trailhead. This trail begins in rocky terrain, crosses washes, ascends through boulder fields, and then winds through oak and pine woodland before concluding with washes and Joshua tree woodland.

Geology Tour Road is an 18-mile drive in Joshua Tree National Park that has sections only accessible to four-wheel drive vehicles. The 18-mile motor tour leads through one of Joshua Tree National Park's most fascinating landscapes. The entire trail is located inside Joshua Tree National Park. It is a long loop trail that is very scenic with beautiful views, surrounding mountains and interesting rock formations.

Author Page

Billy Grinslott & Kinsey Marie Books

Copyright, All Rights Reserved

ISBN – 9781965098219

Thanks

www.ingramcontent.com/pod-product-compliance
Lightning Source LLC
Chambersburg PA
CBHW060850270326
41934CB00002B/83